SPACE JAM
A NEW LEGACY
TUNE SQUAD

By David Lewman
Illustrated by Red Central Ltd

 A GOLDEN BOOK • NEW YORK

Copyright © 2021 Warner Bros. Entertainment Inc.
SPACE JAM: A NEW LEGACY and all related characters and elements
© & TM Warner Bros. Entertainment Inc. WB SHIELD: TM & © WBEI. (s21)

Published in the United States by Golden Books, an imprint of Random House Children's Books, a division of Penguin Random House LLC, 1745 Broadway, New York, NY 10019, and in Canada by Penguin Random House Canada Limited, Toronto. Golden Books, A Golden Book, A Little Golden Book, the G colophon, and the distinctive gold spine are registered trademarks of Penguin Random House LLC.
rhcbooks.com
ISBN 978-0-593-38239-4 (trade) — ISBN 978-0-593-38240-0 (ebook)
Printed in the United States of America
10 9 8 7 6 5 4 3 2

One day in Looney Tunes World, **Bugs Bunny** had a very special visitor: **LeBron James**, the world-famous basketball player! LeBron asked Bugs to help him put together an unbeatable basketball team.

LeBron wanted big, strong players, like Superman.

"I know just who to get!" Bugs said.

First, Bugs needed a vehicle. He had an idea!
He planted a flag in the ground, announcing,
"I declare this land for Planet Earth!"

ZOOM!  A spaceship arrived!

Marvin the Martian got out
and claimed the land for Mars instead!

While Marvin was busy, Bugs borrowed his spaceship.
As his ship blasted off without him, Marvin said,
"You have made me very angry!"

Bugs landed in a giant city and searched for his old pals.
He found **Daffy Duck** . . . who had become Super Duck!
Porky was with him, documenting his heroic misadventures.
But there were already a lot of talented heroes in the city.

Bugs told Daffy if they joined his basketball team,
Daffy would be the team's hero.
"Fine," Daffy agreed. "Dibs on coach!"

Bugs, Daffy, and Porky flew the spaceship to a desert planet. Bugs listened carefully.

BEEP! BEEP!

Road Runner was being chased by
Wile E. Coyote! Two more of their buddies!
Bugs convinced them to join his basketball team.

On a friendly planet, **Sylvester the cat** tried to catch **Tweety**.

"Sufferin' succotash!" he said when Tweety escaped his clutches yet again.

"I tawt I taw a puddy tat!" said Tweety.

Bugs invited his friends to join his team.
They agreed, and Sylvester promised
not to chase Tweety.

Back on the ship,
Bugs and Daffy made
a list of the players
they'd gotten so far.
Including . . .
Elmer Fudd!

Bugs found his old chum **Yosemite Sam** in a café playing piano for a small audience.

Bugs asked, "How'd you like to play basketball in front of millions of cheering fans?"

"Ya got yourself a deal, varmint!"
Yosemite Sam bellowed.

Bugs thought LeBron's team could use at least one really wild player to confuse the other team. So he went looking for **Taz**.

But Bugs didn't have to look far, because Taz came to him!

As the team's coach, Daffy said they needed a player who could provide veteran leadership. Bugs immediately thought of **Granny**. In her long lifetime, she'd seen it all!

Quickness was important, too, so they also recruited
the incredibly fast mouse named **Speedy Gonzales**.
Now the Tune Squad needed only one more player. . . .

Bugs found **Lola Bunny** with the Amazons. "We can't win without you," he told her. "You're our best player!"

Lola hated leaving, but she loved helping her Looney Tunes friends.

"Let's do this!" she cried.

Back in Looney Tunes World, LeBron stared at the players
Bugs had brought him. They did not look big and strong.

"*This* is your unbeatable team?" he asked.

"Yup," Bugs said. "Best in the world!"

LeBron took a deep breath. "Okay," he said. "I'll whip this squad into shape."